Tutu's Quilt · Ke Kapa Kuiki a Tūtū

Remember who you are. Be gracious, but never forget whence you came, for there is where you heart is. This is the cradle of life.

attributed to KING KALĀKAUA [1836–1891]

Tutu's Quilt

Ke Kapa Kuiki a Tūtū

James Rumford

Mānoa Press | Honolulu

2012

Tutu's Quilt
Ke Kapa Kuiki a Tūtū

This edition is based on the 1998 edition entitled *When Silver Needles Swam: The Story of Tūtū's Quilt / Ke Kui Ihe o Tūtū*. With thanks to my editor Leslie Keahiloa Lang, my mentor Harriett Oberhaus, my Hawaiian teacher Puakea Nogelmeier, my friend Sally Jo Bowman, who provided the quote from King Kalākaua, and Lee Wild, who offered valuable information on Hawaiian quilting.

The illustrations were done in watercolor and in pen and ink. The type is Adobe Garamond Pro and the titling is Caslon Openface. Book design is by the author and was done with Adobe InDesign 5.5.

ISBN-13 978-1891839108 (MĀNOA PRESS)
ISBN-10 1891839101

For more information on this book, its creation as well as educational activities, go to:
http://www.jamesrumford.com
http://www.manoapress.com

1 2 3 4 5 6 7 8 9

For my grandmother
Clara Frances Rumford
1882–1971

IN THE 1970s, I saw an interview on television of an ancient Hawaiian woman who remembered the day in 1898, when the flag came down and Hawai'i was annexed to the United States. "No one went out," she said. She went on to tell how everyone stayed inside and closed the windows, even though it was a very hot day. For her and the other Hawaiians, it was a time of mourning.

In 1997, as the hundredth anniversary of annexation neared, I remembered the interview and wrote this story, publishing it the following year under the title *When Silver Needles Swam*. The book soon attracted attention, not just in Hawaiʻi but in the rest of the country as well, and received along with other Hawaiian language books from Mānoa Press the award Nā Manu a Kaʻae from ʻAhahui ʻŌlelo Hawaiʻi for helping to preserve the Hawaiian language.

After a time, the first edition of *When Silver Needles Swam* went out of print. It was not until recently that I decided to republish the book. I changed the title to *Tutu's Quilt*, re-edited portions of the text, and added pictures that did not appear in the original edition. The result is this print-on-demand book.

JAMES RUMFORD
Mānoa, Honolulu
April 19, 2012

Tutu, our grandmother, sat under the breadfuit tree when she quilted. Up and down, in and out, the silver beak of her *ihe* [ee-hay] fish, as she called her needle, swam along the cloth.

Tutu said that the thread was a fishing line, and my sister and I watched as her silver *ihe* fish darted through the 'waves' of the quilt, pulling the thread behind.

Sometimes Tutu would give us pieces of cloth to practice sewing on.

"Careful," she would laugh, "or Ihe might become an eel and bite!"

We'd giggle.

1

Noho ʻo Tūtū ma lalo o ke kumu ʻulu a humuhumu i ke kuiki. I luna, i lalo, i loko, i waho, holo ka nuku hinuhinu o kona iʻa ihe, ʻo ia nō kona inoa no kona kui, ma ke kapa.

Wahi a Tūtū, he ʻaho lawaiʻa ka lopi, a nānā māua ʻo koʻu kaikaina i ka huki ʻana o ka ihe kālā i ka lopi ma hope ona, iā ia e holo ana ma nā ʻale o ke kuiki.

Aia aku eia mai, hāʻawi ʻo Tūtū iā māua i wahi kapa no ka hoʻomaʻamaʻa.

"Akahele o lilo ʻo Ihe i puhi a nahu mai!" i ʻī mai ai ʻo Tūtū me ka ʻakaʻaka.

ʻAkaʻaka pū nō hoʻi māua.

2

Then Tutu would tell stories about how skinny Ihe could change into an eel with sharp teeth and bully his way around the reef. Or how, as a sea urchin, he bristled with needles and warned all to stay away.

But no matter what Ihe turned into, no matter what adventures he had, good or bad, he never forgot who he really was.

———————

A laila haku ʻo Tūtū i nā moʻolelo e pili ana iā Ihe wīwī, ka mea i lilo i puhi me ka niho ʻoʻoi a ʻimi hana aku ʻimi hana mai ma ka hāpapa. Ka mea i lilo auaneʻi i wana me nā kui wanawana ʻoiʻoi a hoʻopale aku hoʻopale mai.

ʻOiai ʻo ia i lilo i mea like ʻole he nui a hana i nā hana wiwoʻole, ʻaʻole i poina ʻo wai lā ia.

A Quilt with Ihe Fish · He Kuiki Ihe

By the end of the story he was glad to be an *ihe* again, darting through the waves of the quilt.

We laughed at Ihe's adventures, but Tutu always ended with: "Be like the *ihe*. Always remember who you are."

Everyone loved Tutu's quilts. Papa, because they felt thin and cool in the summer when the night lizards chirped. Mama, because they felt thick and cozy in the winter when the lizards slept and the wind roared through the palm trees.

A pau ka moʻolelo, hauʻoli ʻo ia e lilo hou i ihe a holo māmā ma lalo o nā ʻale o ke kapa kuiki.

ʻAkaʻaka māua i ka hana wiwoʻole a Ihe, akā hoʻopau mau ʻo Tūtū i ka moʻolelo penei: "E hoʻopili ʻolua iā Ihe. E hoʻomanaʻo mau ʻo wai lā ʻolua."

Aloha nā mea apau i nā kapa kuiki a Tūtū. Wahi a Pāpā, he ʻoluʻolu a lahilahi i ke kau wela, ke kau e kēkēkēkē ai ka moʻo i ka pō. Wahi a Māmā, he mehana a mānoa i ke kau anu, ke kau e moe ai ka moʻo a e nū ai ka makani i nā lau niu.

My sister and I loved them because each quilt had its own special design. Tutu made a strong breadfuit tree for Papa's quilt. For Mama's, she made a beautiful red ginger. But for my sister and me she made butterflies, because, she said, we were always flitting about.

Aloha nō ho'i māua 'o ko'u kaikaina i nā kuiki a Tūtū, no ka mea, ua koho 'ia ka lau o ke kapa e ho'okohu i ke kanaka nona ia kapa. Ho'olālā 'o Tūtū i ke kumu 'ulu ikaika no ko Pāpā kuiki. No ko Māmā, ho'olālā 'ia ka 'awapuhi 'ula'ula nani loa. Akā, no māua me ko'u kaikaina, ho'olālā 'ia nā pulelehua, no ka mea, wahi āna, lelelele nō māua i nā wahi apau.

Tutu's Quilts · Nā Kuiki a Tūtū

 One day, Papa came home with bad news. He and Mama talked in whispers. Then they told Tutu. We stood at the doorway and heard *auē*, the cry of deep sadness.

"Hawai'i has been annexed!"

'Annexed' was a big word. Papa explained that Hawai'i was no longer a country.

"It is part of America now," he said.

There was nothing more to say. Everyone was used to changes. Five years before, the Queen had been arrested and then a republic declared. Now the Republic was gone, and our flag would be taken down.

"We are Americans now," said Papa several weeks later. "It's just as well."

Tutu's *ihe* needle bit into her finger. Was it reminding her of something?

 I kekahi lā, ho'i mai-la 'o Pāpā me ka nūhou 'ino. Hāwanawana lāua 'o Māmā, A laila 'ōlelo aku-la lāua me Tūtū. Ma ka 'īpuka, lohe maila māua: "Auē! Auē nō ho'i ē! Ua ho'ohui 'ia aku nei ka 'āina!"

'A'ole i maopopo iā māua, a wehewehe maila 'o Pāpā, "I kēia manawa, 'a'ole he au-puni 'o Hawai'i. Pili ia iā 'Amelika."

'A'ole 'ōlelo 'ana i koe. Ua ma'a nā kānaka i ka nūhou 'ino. 'Elima makahiki ma mua, ua hopu 'ia ka Mō'ī Wahine, a laila kūkala 'ia ka lepupalika. A i kēia manawa nō, ua nalo ka Lepupalika, a e huki 'ia iho auane'i ko kākou hae.

"He 'Amelika kākou," mea mai 'o Pāpā ma hope o kekahi mau pule. "E aho paha ia."

Nahu ihola ko Tūtū kui ihe i kona ma-namanalima. He hana ho'omana'o paha ia hana a ke kui?

"You'll soon see, my little leis."
"E maopopo ana, e aʻu mau lei."

The next day, as the American warship *Philadelphia* steamed into Honolulu harbor, Tutu called to my sister and me. "My little blossoms, we're going into town today."

We were excited. And when Tutu took down her red tin savings box, we knew we were off to buy something very important. But nothing we did could get Tutu to tell us what she was going to buy.

"You'll soon see, my little leis," she said.

———————

I ia lā a'e, i ka hiki 'ana o ka moku kaua 'Amelika *Philadelphia*, mea mai 'o Tūtū, "E a'u mau pua, hele pū kākou i ke kaona."

A ki'i 'o Tūtū i kāna pahu kini 'ula, 'o ko māua ho'omaopopo ihola nō ia, ke hele nei mākou e kū'ai i kekahi mea nui. Nalu aku nalu mai māua me ka nīnau aku i kāna mea e kū'ai mai.

"E maopopo ana, e a'u mau lei."

 At Ah Sing's Dry Goods, Tutu bought several yards of white muslin and the last bits of red and blue cloth in the shop.

"Mama, you lucky get red and blue cloth," the Chinese man said in broken Hawaiian. "Everybody making American flags for celebration at Palace tomorrow. Big fireworks at night, too!"

Tutu just smiled. Back in the street, my sister and I pestered her with questions: "Are we making an American flag? Will we see the fireworks? Why do we need so many *ihe* fish needles?"

"You'll soon see, my little butterflies."

When we got back home, Tutu carefully cut the red, white and blue cloth into strips until it was too dark to work.

Ma ka hale kūʻai o Ah Sing i kūʻai mai ai ʻo Tūtū i pahu kui me nā iā he nui o ke keʻokeʻo maoli a me nā ʻapana hope loa o ke kapa ʻula a me ka polū.

Mea mai ka Pakē me ka pāhemahema ʻana i ka ʻōlelo: "E Māmā, lāki ʻoe, loaʻa kapa ʻula kapa polū. Hana kānaka apau i hae ʻAmelika no hoʻolauleʻa ma ʻIolani ʻapōpō. Nui nō hoʻi ahikao i ka pō."

Ua minoʻaka wale ʻo Tūtū. Ma ke alanui,

ua noke māua i ka nīnau: "E hana ana kākou i ka hae ʻAmelika? E ʻike ana kākou i ke ahikao? No ke aha lā e pono ai i kēnā mau kui ihe he nui?"

"E mōakāka ana, e aʻu mau pulelehua."

A ma ka hale, ua paʻahana ʻo Tūtū i ka ʻoki mōlina ʻana i ka lole ʻula, keʻokeʻo a me ka polū a hiki i ka mōlehulehu.

That night, my sister and I whispered under our butterfly quilt, wondering what Tutu was going to make.

By morning, the white muslin was spread out under the breadfruit tree. A neat pile of red, white and blue strips lay to the side. It was plain to see that Tutu was making a quilt. But what was the design going to be?

My sister and I watched as Tutu began pinning the strips of cloth to the muslin. Curious, Papa and Mama came over to see. Tutu put down more strips.

Even though this was the day of the big celebration, none of the neighbors were planning to go. Instead, they came by to watch Tutu. Soon there was a small crowd.

I ka pō, hāwanawana ihola māua ma lalo o ke kuiki pulelehua, me ka nūnē aku nūnē mai, he aha lā kāna hana.

A ao, ua hāliʻi ʻia ka lole keʻokeʻo ma lalo o ke kumu ʻulu, a aia ma ka ʻaoʻao he puʻu nani o nā mōlina ʻula, keʻokeʻo a me ka polū. Ua mōakāka, ua mākaukau ʻo Tūtū e kuiki kapa. Akā he aha kona lau?

Iā māua e kiʻei ana, hoʻopaʻa ihola ʻo Tūtū i nā mōlina ma luna o ke kapa me ka pine. Ua niele ʻo Pāpā lāua ʻo Māmā a hele mai e nānā. Pine hou ʻo Tūtū i nā mōlina.

ʻO kēia ka lā o ka hoʻolauleʻa nui, ʻaʻole naʻe makemake nā hoa noho e hele. Ma kahi o ka hele ʻana, kipa maila lākou e ʻike iā Tūtū. A ma hope koke iho, aia he pōʻai o ka poʻe.

16

As Tutu put down the last strips, we saw that she had made a design of Hawaiian flags. Then for the center of the quilt, she made a lei of these words in yellow: *ku'u hae aloha,* 'my beloved flag.'

Someone saw the little box of needles and began passing them around. Soon everyone—including my sister and me—began sewing.

A i ka pine 'ana i nā mōlina hope loa, 'o ko mākou 'ike ihola nō ia i ka lau kuiki: 'o ka hae Hawai'i. 'O kona hana ihola nō ia i lei melemele me kēia mau 'ōlelo: ku'u hae aloha.

Wehe ihola kekahi i ka pahu li'ili'i o nā kui a hā'awi aku. Ho'omaka ihola nā mea apau—'o māua 'o ko'u kaikaina kekahi—e humuhumu.

17

People would call it a miracle.
ʻŌlelo ʻia, he hana mana kēia hana.

Our needles truly became *ihe* fish, swimming in silvery schools through the layers of cloth.

By evening, the quilt was finished. Later people would call it a miracle, for no quilt could be made in a day.

"I will sleep under my flag tonight," Tutu said, embracing each one and thanking them for their aloha.

After it got dark, we went outside to see the fireworks.

When, at last, the night was quiet again, Tutu called us back inside.

Ua lilo wale nā kui ihe hinuhinu o mākou i iʻa kū a holo ma nā ʻale o ke kapa.

A ahiahi aʻela, ua pau ke kuiki ʻana. Ma hope, ua ʻōlelo nā kānaka he hana mana kēia hana, no ka mea, he mea kūpanainaha ka hoʻopau ʻana i ke kuiki i hoʻokahi wale nō lā.

"E hiamoe ana au ma lalo o kuʻu hae i kēia pō," i ʻōlelo ai ʻo Tūtū me ka honi ʻana i nā kānaka pākahi, me ka mahalo nō hoʻi i ko lākou aloha.

A pōʻeleʻele, hele akula māua i waho e ʻike i ke ahikao.

A laʻi hou ka pō, kāhea maila ʻo Tūtū iā māua e hoʻi i loko o ka hale.

The flag quilt was on her bed.

"You will become Americans and learn their language and their ways," she said. "But one day, this quilt will be yours—to comfort you and remind you of today."

Then she kissed us, whispering in our ears, "Be like the *ihe*. Always remember who you are."

Aia ma kona wahi moe ke kuiki hae.

Mea mai ʻo Tūtū, "E lilo ana ʻolua i mea ʻAmelika. E aʻo ana ʻolua i kā lākou ʻōlelo me ko lākou loina. I kekahi lā, no ʻolua kēia kapa kuiki. He mea hōʻoluʻolu ia. He mea hoʻomanaʻo i kēia lā nō hoʻi."

A honi maila ʻo Tūtū iā māua me ka hāwanawana mai, "E hoʻopili ʻolua i ka ihe. E hoʻomanaʻo mau nō ʻo wai lā ʻolua."

Be like the ihe.

E hoʻopili ʻolua i ka ihe.

In the middle of the nineteenth century, the American missionaries taught Hawaiians how to make quilts. Before long, Hawaiians began creating quilts with appliqué designs. These designs were usually of tropical plants, but in the last half of the nineteenth century, as Hawai'i began losing its independence, a new design appeared: the Hawaiian flag. And when Hawai'i was annexed to the United States in 1898,

more and more flag quilts appeared. Some said it was because Hawaiians still wanted to sleep under their own flag.

The story you have just read takes place between July 13, 1898, when news of annexation reached Hawai'i, and August 12, 1898, when the Hawaiian flag was taken down at 'Iolani Palace. During that month, as American dignitaries aboard the warship

Philadelphia *made their way to Honolulu, newspapers were filled with ads selling American flags and fireworks for the August 12th festivities. But, on that day, most Hawaiians stayed home to mourn the passing of their country.*

Hawai'i is the only state in the Union that was once a modern nation. Although Texas and California might claim to have been nation states, they were short-lived republics, ruled by ex-patriot Americans. Hawai'i, on the other hand, was a modern nation ruled by Hawaiians until 1893. Its affairs were conducted in Hawaiian, and its values were deeply rooted in the past. All this changed when the monarchy was overthrown in 1893, and change became irreversible when Hawai'i was annexed.

I wrote this book to explore what it would be like to lose one's country and flag. I created a Hawaiian family to show what effect annexation would have on them.

First there is the shock of the news. Then when the father accepts the loss of his country, the grandmother is determined to make sense of events for herself and for her granddaughters. She also has her eye on her neighbors. While she cannot stop annexation, she can remind all around her that in the face of change, they must remember who they are and where they have come form. To do this, Grandmother turns to two ancient Hawaiian values: aloha *and* alu like *(pulling together). Like her ancestors who came to these uninhabited islands, Grandmother has landed, in a sense, on a new island, ruled by Americans. If they are to survive, they must remember how to love one another and how to work together. They must remember what made them great in the past and what will hold them together in the future.*

Tūtū and her family slept under their quilts, but many Hawaiians did not. A Hawaiian quilt was a thing of beauty, made with loving hands and the product of months of hard work. As for flag quilts, these were usually put away and shown only on special occasions.

Tūtū *is the Hawaiian word for* "grandparent." *The* ihe *(also* ihehihe *or* meʻemeʻe*) is the half-beak fish and is related to flying fish.* Aloha *is untranslatable. It can mean love, mercy, compassion, kindness, not to mention hello and good-bye.*

With thanks to my editor Leslie Keahiloa Lang, my mentor the late Harriett Oberhaus, my Hawaiian teacher Puakea Nogelmeier, and Lee Wild, who provided valuable information on Hawaiian quilting.

Other books by James Rumford:

The Cloudmakers
The Island-below-the-Star
Seeker of Knowledge
Traveling Man
Ka-hala-o-puna
Calabash Cat
There's a Monster in the Alphabet
Nine Animals and the Well
Dog-of-the-Sea-Waves
Sequoyah
Don't Touch My Hat!
Beowulf
Silent Music
Chee-Lin
Rain School
Mango Rain
Beo-Bunny [forthcoming]
Standing Tall [forthcoming]
From the Good Mountain [forthcoming]
Island below the Star [forthcoming]
Z [forthcoming]
For more information, please visit:

http://www.jamesrumford.com